The Parts of Light

JOHNS HOPKINS:
POETRY AND FICTION

John T. Irwin, General Editor

This book has been brought to publication with the generous
assistance of the Albert Dowling Trust.

The Johns Hopkins University Press
2715 North Charles Street
Baltimore, Maryland 21218-4319
The Johns Hopkins Press Ltd., London

Library of Congress Cataloging-in-Publications Data will be found
at the end of this book.
A catalog record for this book is available from the British Library.

ISBN 0-8018-4939-X
ISBN 0-8018-4940-3 (PBK)

THE

Parts

OF

Light

Poems by

VICKI

HEARNE

The Johns Hopkins University Press

Baltimore and London

For Robert Tragesser

CONTENTS

The Parts of Light

BETWEEN FENCES

for John Hollander

And then discussed with the horse
The attributes of God, made
Peace with them. This was called

Pace between fences, was judged
For balance on turns, because
The flying changes, treasured

From the start, had been marked out
As one excellence against
The gruffer idolatries.

The horse was civil but liked
To discuss God and still does,
Changing leads from right to left,

Engaging fully the stout
Haunches. The change is analyzed
As shifts in the count of hooves, is

No optical illusion:
What we cannot see is not
There to be seen but the ground

Keeps the pace between fences
Steady until the new fence
Looms up; reason arches

Firmer than all our prayers, and takes charge.

The horse is the largest animal
of love so

is the bluebird
                    and the logician
who did not doubt stones may
have been kind to them
for all he knew.   This shows up

in the way words
face into infinity when they do, finding
the other in the vast gleam
of exteriority and it is
a brave affair like the blemished badge
of justice that does not protect the heart even

as the horse holds his stand and the cop
while the contraband air riots.

                        Or I could say that truth halts
at road signs, right or wrong. Horsemen
speak of balance at the halt; knowledge picks
through the wood crowded with the glitter and glitz,
gigantic, of all knowledge is not and must learn
balance at the halt which is a matter
of motion because horses as they instruct spook

first and answer questions
later knowing themselves
as generous surfaces.

The section of the old army manual
about traversing the minefield said to drop the reins,
give your horse his head and that's one map
of know-how: True pace

is the collected extension
from which beauty flies everywhere as your mount settles
in the poise of self carriage.

During the dark of the moon
(Now, as you nod at your book
In lamplight) a sober-winged owl

Eyes the moon as both remain
Out of sight. Thus moon and owl
Converse, keeping the ocean

Tides, moon and owl aloft there
As we, our eyes as high up
Over the book as need be, keep

The gods, like us, aloft.   Our
Words on the wind wrap the world
In august conversations,

Human speaking intersects
The path to the void, the light
In its fractions, and the sun

And the sun's opposite star's
Mystery of water pours
Untidy, chilly knowledge

Out like a benificence.

TO THE CIRCUS

for Diana Starr Cooper

Everything is swing: The horses' necks
Swing smoothest in their curved point to point,
The trapezes easiest for us

To build stories toward. The elephants'
Trunks make a move, like philosophers
Who are just about to understand.

Let's skip the part where the trapezists
Fall, the elephants are put to work
Too young, the circus folk too old, too

Doomed: It is there, it is noted, it
Will never matter here where the scent,
Embedded with sequins, is how life

Smells to tall, ardent children who tug
In the middle of a plenitude
Where even stray pragmatists find God,

Shuddering at how God loves our flares.

The knowledge of this horse arises
As a tall fence, mighty oxer, a
Trappy ditch, a green deceptive bank

The horses know better through ascents
The ground trembles under the way love
Trembles to hear her name, the way love

Trembles to call her name. The fox knows
How to leave the horses behind, how
Darting over water is a daring

Not undone by hounds, and how darkness
Is not dark in the flews of a hound.
The hounds, becomingly inured to heats

Ignorance spells out in the shadows,
Read off security there, and grace
Is a beastly manner of knowledge,

Readiness another, flight also
Another. Trust far and wide—as far
And wide the wit and wander and wing

Lift of the falcon sways over her
Way of softening the air until
She can get through to survival. Trust

Us, who know ourselves, for whom nothing
Else will serve, mark out, awkward as wit
Clogged with death, each graciousness of beast.

Each graciousness of beast not to be
What we are. The selves of our horses
Settle, more simultaneous, more

Bright than love, over every brush thick
Scent in the summer, over every stone
Thin thought in the winter and settle

Over us who cannot know them, can
Know no more than the sour sufferings
Intended by the skin's boundaries.

Our eyes harden against the heartsick
Distinction between dying and death
Wisdom structures as warning, as if

To wither against acquaintanceship
Were to encode our wants against air,
The refuse of denial our towns

Contemplate until: Cathedrals vault
Like children or equations taking
Our breasts with them so that we can lift

Ourselves as artifice, as fated
After all as the fox and the hound
Are to be, free selves equal to worlds.

The graces of human consciousness
Forbid what is fleeter, cannier
Than our compliant and clumsiest

Frettings, for this is what was given
Even to our fingertips, their pluck
On guitar, lute, harp and beloved—

And the mind of Shakespeare, though missing
In action, is said to have survived
Our return to the inert grid of thought.

REMEMBERING A SHATTERED
GLASS HORSE

Take away a dimension (the third,
Not the fourth) and call what you have left
A horizon, a length along which

The sand—there would be sand—coasted up
Down or around from that figuring
Scribble—letters from your lover,

Or of your nickname. Now watch them break
The clean line of the horizon before
You are halfway done. Whatever leaps

From the debris to form the armchair
Across from the window outside of
Which—oh, horses graze roughly the bounds

Of vague grasses, some of which nourish—
That is the world. The scribbled letters?
All those cogent improprieties?

The eloquence of your proper name.

HUCK FINN, CREDULOUS AT THE CIRCUS

To be gulled, even in the afternoon
Of reason, into a belief
In the sudden access of sobriety

Conferred on the clown by the lithe voltes,
Mistaken caprioles of the liberty
Of horses—to be so gulled

Was to watch from the shadows,
Evading again the town as
Revealed in the burnt-black sun, and blink

In the glare of knowledge, in a light
Falsely thickened by scoundrels
Of revealing. The ringmaster, sharp

With artistry, unfolded his face
In the shape of logic and cleared up
The act and bowed. Who but the squinting

Vagrant boy would fear for the rider
When the rider leaped, when his head was in
The show, actual beneath the shift of hooves?

THE SECRET IS SAFE IN JERUSALEM

for Colleen Mendelsohn

I have wounds but no authority. I confided
My wounds to Jerusalem once
We were alone together, trusting
That for all of her light the secret
Was safe with her. For we were alone
Together, Intifada had emptied
Her markets, beloved, said Rilke,
Of God. The markets empty: in Jerusalem

My hand is not wounded, my mouth is not wounded, only
My heart stumbles slowly. We have wounds
But no authority.   In Kentucky

I walked on blue grass, touched blue
Horses where nothing was in flames.   Kentucky
Is beautiful because flame
Is enjoined there are no stones

Allotted to lie in the paths of the horses
Striking sparks from their hooves whose hearts
Must not stumble, the horses who are bold
Among the soft grasses.   Jerusalem
Is beautiful because flame-proof, and there
Is no drought and no song and no flinty
Hesitation of the throat, sparks
Ignite neither the walls nor the uneven
Rubble nor the inflammable syllables.   Because Job

Listened to the voice that said so, praising
The horse for the way his head
Lifted to hear the shouting of the captains, the way
Thunder became the invisible cloak
Of his throat, the conflagration

Stops here, must stop here.   In Jerusalem
I am not wounded and because there my wounds give me
No authority, no grievance, I shall forget her
Whose inhabitants play with fire.   I shall dream

Of Kentucky whose grass plays
Heedlessly under the glancing hooves of yearlings,
Whose stallions exact deluxe forgetful dances from us,

Whose grief is guarded on Mount Zion.   In Jerusalem

I am not wounded, and because here my wounds give me
No authority I have forgotten
Whose inhabitants play with fire. If there is justice

The secret is safe. Let it stay safe. Let nothing
Mar the perfect pink stones
Of Jerusalem, the perfect blue grass of Kentucky,
The inadvertent foals who have unwounded grace
Bound in their grass-soft authority.

Not when they stick in your throat
Like fighters but when blankets
Lie over the mind in summer.

Stone walls in the daytimes go
Away and the horses there
Vanish in a stale air-mash,

Dreams rounded out on the tongue,
Everything so much improved
There is no thing anywhere,

No young dapple gray at all,
No exacting bite of him,
His hooves measuring the air—

Grounds rough enough for life.

They say you never forget
So you had sure better not
But you do. The light chuckles

To hear this, chuckles out loud
As you pick up your courage
With the reins. That's what happens

When you pick up the reins, legs
Better remember! because
Riding is remembering

To ask politely. The horse
May tell you her stable name,
Then the one she dances by,

Or may not, but if she does
The light stops its mocking,
Gets going on the smooth streets

Of the world. The horse's scope,
The confident cathedrals,
Allow truth its say as if

Riding were remembering.

When ease comes the classic horse's hooves
Roughen the ground so in their spring hard
Prayers that for a moment everything

Is visible; words lie all before
The relaxed landscape. Cramped up to peer
Through the miracles of landscape we see

Instead and become the patina
Of the holy cities as blood widens
Like love, especially in Hebrew . . .

Truth is like that when for brief moments
At a time we see forever and
The light at last is good for nothing

From the need-bound darkness, from the long
Stumble of the horses over all
In an instant in the startled air.

When death comes horses are not like this.
Their heads lengthen, their teeth from calling
Form rectangular swirls as the fall

Of the air tears, gives their teeth away.

The mind, an apparatus, meets up
With the world and measures this and that,
Praises the other thing, the odd thing,

The lime-green leaf. The chittering birds
Fly wide in the body's dance; the soul
Loves body and mind, is indiscreet.

As human and dog pass on the street
Without remark, the sun blushes dark,
Backs into the deep. The gallant birds,

Blue and green, sing the sun into place
Again, after the dream, while the soul,
Stretching at the window pane, approves.

Remark to your red-bone hound how gay
The frost you crash through is, put off blood,
Let creation graze, let the nubbed pull

Of day remind you that thought lives on
In the bones and branches, and prayer
Runs like sap, get out your red-bone hound—

(Red-bone, blue tick, part coyote they say)—
Make the mind speak with no dull measure,
Let the soul with noise approve the sun.

Why he wanted the mountain? What in
The ground failed to support the right airs
Above ground? On he runs, and as he

Runs his footsteps shatter the sand's crust
And remain where they are. Behind him
And before him the laws of form fall,

Fall. The mountain retreats, big and gay
In a remote diction of gesture,
Diction of a space that figures forth

Hyperboles of separation—
The mountain's vehement expression
Of gaps no stride can measure. He reads

This, reads in the didactic air want
Of mountains and runs on, a gnostic
In the ignorant wilderness until

His foot lands square on time, then hovers
Where bare Elements meet the singing
Shell of prophesy and there embrace,

Figuring forth possible mountains
Of form. He is taken up, caressed,
Enclosed within the mountain's pleasure.

When it transpired that the meaning
Drifting in the limbs of the young dog was
Eclipsable, like any old light, some
Learned a new
Name for God, some garbled
Older inscriptions already worn

By the softness of wringing
Words, hands, notes, cries into crevices
In place of significance.
                                    Trapped in infinite
Light we cannot pronounce
Its name, but Goethe,
Dying, could.

Dogs do dance.   Not a trick of the light but
The light.   What is left over
Vanishes like our helplessness
As when the gazelles after a last flash
Disappear before we can trace
On air the shapes of our mouths
We take for explanation.

ION, RELEASED FROM THE VOWS
OF LOVE, REPLIES TO SOCRATES

I can only stand and look, my friend,
And tell the tale of Proteus
Again. The shapes you see when my gaze

Holds yours are you because Proteus
Is a mirror, time is a mirror,
You and I and the sun are mirrors.

The poet tells how a leopard sprang
From the eyes of desire; in this
We see the truth that will not make sense

For she loves us beyond our reasons
For inquiring, she replies to us
As the sea replies to the moon's long

Philosophies of motion. My craft
Lies in knowing this far too swiftly
To tell you. It is knowledge that weeps,

The diaspora of the goddess
Whose faith lives in our love of the sun,
Whose gray eyes regard us from the hill.

HOLOCAUST POEM

The beauty of children is to shine
Forth creamier than roses colored
Like silk; there is no human failure.

Arthritic pianists have flawless
Memories for cadenzas. Colts
Prance well within the economies

Of good taste. The geldings of Paris
Have never quarreled with their wives who
Have flawless memories of manhood.

The proof of our errors lies in love.

Some days the damp
storms about
consume the mountains
late and rough hewn

as we wear
clothes in the wind or
summer's heat bears down
on skin that wants

to be free and we wear
gay clothes anyway
for guidance and the other's eyes
see our clothes and from there

move to our eyes and back
or ankles participating
expressively in our stride:
the animals do not

wear clothes whether
or not they need to, they
express the weather, we
wear clothes because we can

dance in them, gesture
from storm to sun
and to eyes, it is
something like a poem.

The problem of knowing is inscribed
In the condition of controlled air
The curators provide through which the hand

Gestures from a horse's haunch to lines
That in a shoulder bend to the haunch
But in their own plane on an incline.

Your hand gestures plane to plane, place
To place, taking time about it all,
This way knowing, this way in doubt

Of infinite planes that intersect
Such a mass of rambunctious horse,
Robustness of horseman, that my eye

Knows them through your hand. Just so: the truth
Grasped in the well-timed museum air
Here for the flat canvas, knows your hand.

The hand of thought swivels, parrying
In turn, pausing to catch up, more street
Light, more kinds of shadow than the face

God or Beloved show. The eye knows
What it sees, through to them both. The hand
Thinks in the streaks of dark artists push

Through charcoal and the brightest oil and
Marble dust to brush off seeing, felt
In a blocky paradox. To tell:

First the hand and then the mind retreat
From our appeal to them to tell how
They tell numbers and cat's cradles, some

Values on an abacus. We face
The numberless quiet of the hand's
Thrust in the iridescent edges

Of what the world knows without our help—
Not ideas—but how can a hand
Leave itself alone, blind with no grasp

Of its own subtle pillars? Through them
Is completion of body and town,
 Statues inscribed by a shaky grasp

On the Nikon that will spill it all,
Reveal the hold. Helped by our gawking
The hand shows up its separate sense.

TOUCH OF CLASS
OR
VIEW FROM WITHIN ANY
IMPERIAL RIDING ACADEMY

In these mere scenes and landscapes
Dilettantes prefer, what blurs is

Becoming as truth entranced,
Formed before No and Yes, before

The choice between opulence
And laughter. In this mare's leaps

We count the ripples spreading
From God's joy that this mare's legs

Make ripples no matter who
Understands landscapes. The hooves

Of horses touch the spellbound
Throats of new constellations:

They shine with benevolence
As if nature thought about

How geometry loves us.

INSTRUCTIONS FROM A TRAINER
FOR BUILDING A CHARM FOR THE
RECOVERY OF HEALTH

Think of how Eclipse did it, how he studied
With every stride ignorance that kept his hooves
Thrusting thrusting into the most brittle airs
Fluid around his heart, hooves.   Now, having thought
Of Eclipse, glance to your right at the letter
Of damage that lies open on the table
By the crushed face of the moon.   "It is stated
On the label of Eclipse that his spine is undamaged
But this is not so." The curator in white
Has nothing else to say and time becomes you
To call out. To Eclipse, I mean, and not the
Distracting vanishing point off to the right
Of the rubbing down house at Newmarket Heath.
Eclipse may, may not answer. No one else will.

SERENDIPITY

My mouth full of nubbed silk, wild grains
Sort over my tongue into syllables
Cast by the shining whose spills

Darken our homes tolerably. No wonder
We never talk anymore but there are the grains
Breezing up into meaning because you hummed

That morning and invited all the minstrels in,
Shook out the velvet eyes, fed them and were fed
To find me listening. Around the late streets

Striations of light that were bones bump
Into melody, break up the music
Again as though the desire for speech

Catalogued the subject, and matters.

True rhythm is
not hobbled, constrained
by beauty rather. Truth

follows as smoothly
as the forelegs
sing at trot with
the horse when the horse
becomes a cadence

better than leaves become
spring in the action
more brilliant than gold bridled
knowledge. Alchemies

of a long *haute école*
swiften in the sequence
of steps, shift *passage*
to trot and back
to *capriole*, fast

in joy bound hooves
motion lifted by meaning.
Seasons falter as if change
were death while the art

constrained beauty curves
in the figures of desire
inspired, at rest.

The measured horse found the turn
And made it, through
Arabian deserts into Virginian pastures, then

Galleries of motion, calm thought
Restored in articulation. Here the horse insists,

With some success, on her legs
And carries us on,
                          and a studio
Locates announcements of her

Disjunct then recompleted in metals
That trace the bare

Hide of the matter, bones
Of knowledge. The horse insists

That the news she drums out
Moves on and the artist agrees

With some success, insists
On her eyes;
                    the horse scans
The earth which will prove
Too swift for her. The artist

Of the creatures who prove swift
For her finds the turn

Anyway and makes it through.

So each reality follows on
Reality slowed,

Steadied, and finally firm
Enough to walk around.

IF I COULD SPEAK TO CHIEF JOSEPH
ABOUT APPALOOSAS

I would ask how much his bones still
In the darkness know of the fate

Of his horses, pony-tough and these days
Elegant as Thoroughbreds but still

Immune to the spirit bullies, uninsultable and not caring,
Moving quietly off to their dark plateau
From which they view the inwardness
Of the Palouse

Which is enraptured by the ever-renewed song
Of its name dance: Don't-Push-The-River-
And-Don't-Sell. Once I heard a woman

Exclaim in tinny rage that Appaloosas
Are "savage and stupid" by which she indicated

That they turned, as implacable and ruthless
As ponies, away from the false fences, the false standards

Her hands ragged in their mouths coaxed them toward,

And I would send him a snapshot of my Appy caught
Saying, "Look, you can get off right now
Or come along for the ride, if you like,

But I'm doing this my way," and he did,
Clearing fences the way comets

Clear the heavens, and how that horse
Could love a wall! and in this a horse chooses his fate
When it is pressed on him, there is such a thing as a horse
Fated to echo the name dance of Tu-eke-kas,
Thunder-traveling-to-loftier-Mountain-Heights,

Wanting no praise but his own power,
His intimacies with his iron-hard hooves.

And I would tell Chief Joseph that I am white,
Soft bellied these days, but I learned something from that horse
About how to go along for the ride, and if Chief Joseph heard me,

Then I would know what his bones know of the depths,
Going along there for the ride.

SOME GENERAL PRINCIPLES OF THE ART OF RIDING

I.

First to consider are cadence, suppleness,
The lightness of great skill
Which is control, which
Disappears into
        ease:

This requires great labor of preparation
And cannot be sought,
It must be waited for

    Thus the way to ride at spread fences is to create
        impulsion   impulsion

Not speed and
        wait
      don't panic
      this is the hardest thing
          HOW

Do you stay with a pony that can just about
         jump out
            of his skin?

   sound skills
    pretty chilly
     little moves
      let him do his thing

Look at Mary Chapot, tough to beat
With natural tact on White Lightning
        splitting the difference
          winning the cup

II.

The novice stands before a balance of masters
Properly abject but not bowed, the head must be up
Not to repeat errors of technique, thus

   We are grateful
   (all of you)

      to Colonel D'Endrody

       writing his thesis while captive
       at the foot of the Caucasus Mountains
       on the shore of the Black Sea
       where he did no riding

Grisone wrote well but he is deplored
For heavy hands, rigid control
From which the horse soon escapes back
              into
            your
          lap,
              Grisone used
          elaborate bits, numerous tricks
          that have no place in the
                    ART

III.

Yes, there are devices which can be used
                              with great caution
                              by a Rider

Who has learned to evaluate the importance of various
                                        MOVEMENTS
By "feeling"
                    this is a delicate matter
Not beginning
When a pupil knows one trot from the other by clues
Or can count the feet, striking to canter:

                    The student stands
                    At the threshold of art
                         when compelled
By the true stride of every horse
                         he happens to find is his mount.

IV.

Paris:
Pessoa on Gran Geste
A genuine artist, sophisticated,
Cerebral, memorably
Revealing his supple elegance

Tempting us to take foolish chances

Most of us should remain absolutely quiet in the air
                              flight
Is largely a gift from the horse

V.

Notice Steinkraus
Proving to Europeans in their own saddles that Americans
Still transcend and ride

He warns
      that at crucial moments when
       forward movement on a line
               or turn
                     is lost
                        it is
    a great mistake we all make to want to pay
         attention to the
              head when
                  the real solution
   lies in summoning
        the liveliness
            that comes from the rear

THE PROBLEM OF THE
DANCING HORSE

With gaiety say
what our music provokes
say that a waltz

tunes us up so we
say the horse—
who is gay—dances

with say pride parades
what is prior
in his sinews (out

to our pastures of thought
and all along
the daylong walls

in the Academy say
while the landscape winks
like the skeptic with

denial of the hall
in Vienna that means
horses dancing)

The Word was one thing, clear song,
Until language, day seven
That was, or so Nietzsche said,

Became amusement disguised
As something we must languish
Without—language as a noise

Of refusal, all song gone,
All agreement between Word
Work Beauty Praise.   Diatribe

Became duty, tribal thrust,
Weapons of bright righteousness
And no good came of it, none,

Though our poems bear up under
Morality as only
They can, taking that black weight

From our astonished shoulders,
Bearing the leisure of God
As if they had chosen to

However careless of love
Truth might be, or however
Profligate in her revenge.

SELF DECEPTION

We could be a tree
from whom the snow hides
the earth? but nothing
is hidden even when the roots
don't know this. The roots—

The point is the roots
don't hide from the tree
whatever we prefer
summer and winter
not to know. If we could

deceive ourselves, believe
a contradiction, snow
on ourselves, we would be
to blame but are
instead beautiful as we believe

in love by fire love
by ice, love in meadows,
believe in rooms and out of them
go toward and away
at once, live in motion

knowing everything that we know
by contradiction—truth
is like this: a dog leaps
knowing the heavens by gravity's
propositions of lowering.

In our yard, the motley's gone, bruises
Left from Autumn's fading eradicated
When winter traced the bleak landscape.

A wonderland! "Lace" doesn't say it—
What did I know until I knew this,
With of course dutiful worry

About ambulances that do not
Make it through in what might have been
Time and, in keener and less worthy

Worry—what if it were me? Inland,
There is storm. There it is serious.
But how can we be? It is not us.

No creature freezes, no human starves
Though the pleasure of it unnerves us
As the eternal Spouse thinks to say,

"Oh, oh love, our own woods, how beautiful."

One return, granted on a terrace:

Across the mosaics, only human
Voices failed to rise to the marvel
Of a January studded

With oranges. The imported tales
I learned to read from would instruct me
In canonical months, calendars

Of illegible frosts, airs whose names
Could not mean what that valley revealed
In bare songs. I praised thought among fruits

Thoughtless of how winters named in songs
Whose rhymes I would never learn by heart
Approached me. (The fruits! Their humming gleam!)

Orange burnished decorum, natural
As it seemed, would be historied
Out of my sight even by divine

Voices whose exacting praises find
My ears here where the white tile figures
Rebuke my failure to rise, marvel.

Color studded trees now shape the grounds
Of January whose husbandmen
Have calendars literal with fruit.

There's happiness that shatters
In one breath and in that breath
Reforms wider, in the way

The suns of any season
Speak from the leaves, how we
Know leaves. There is light meant

To be known and starlight where
The gay clatter, the glitter
Of winter at rest, is ours.

That is just the happiness
Of the large happiness hearts
Are, speeding, slowing, staying

Steady, as often they do
Under stress of soft feathers,
Sharp ones, pelts fenced with fur

Or unfenced, smoothed by such airs.

The head of the mongoloid child bobs
On its stalk; the sun

Is nearly that graceful, that
Splendid. The child considers

Ways to move across the lawn. Jonquils
On her brilliant path stand

Before her and she moves to
Step elsewhere but moves

Through them instead like speech
Lurching. Speech moves headlong

Through our throats and language
Is as lovely as a child, we are

As mindless as jonquils, the sun
Is nearly that graceful.

GRASSHOPPERS

Children cup their hands
over them and hold

keenly still against
the plump and

Pop
of their flight. It matters

to let go
quickly for the rhythm

of the thing, capture
and grasping are

release as
with thought

such as grasshoppers
think of poignant

accuracy of angles
against the palms, the grass

or the word against
the concave of the throat.

ON THE GROUNDS OF THE STATEWIDE AIR POLLUTION RESEARCH CENTER

seeing a rabbit
I ached into each
detail brown
and gray
and white fur, red
vital veins in
translucent ears, we

stayed still
rabbit and I
stopped by the
sun and air but

when I reached
for my pen
to write it

rabbit scurried
away shuddering
the bushes

THE DOG AND THE WORD

The catechism of dogs
is to attack
at a word, laugh

at another, so
it has been written
so consider

the flash of a Golden
Retriever, mouth so swift
on the pheasant, prairie

chicken, stick or ball, bit
of twine, so
tender, this divine

seizure that wants nothing more
for itself, stands
to deliver and reveals

in the bird dog's celebrant
profile the sky
to the naked eye.   Grab

without greed, we
have no noun
for it, only

the one command.

Dignity: (rare but not obsolete) a
Great Dane, an Irish Wolfhound, a curve
of neck and thigh, graciousness
bowing to our disgrace,
the Dane survives

calumny and is the pride
of the *gebrauchshundesrassen,* the
noble group.

The Wolfhound's humor, no
malice only rosiness
as of a comfortable heart,

can take down wolves, which is how we know
wolves are the enemy.
                                        Giants
Of forebearance, they think
with their chests and their thinking rides
the cathedral scope of their limbs. They breathe

in and breathe back the air
to nourish us. This is their gift,
a talent possessed

by other dogs, mastered
by these friends
of any landscape.

BIRDY QUESTIONS

The question, quick and birdy
As a hot young Pointer in
Tent on the high glamour hills

Seed the air with at dawn, hurts
The mind with heedless romping
Before it learns manners, the

Movements of state. Courtesy
Comes as if knowledgeably
To the field where the sun

Lights the brush as if value
Were visible as the dogs
Become verbs for sudden vision.

It is not for everyone.
Even in the field these Pointers
With golden eyes presaging

Birds are too abruptly here,
Too abruptly gone again,
As if death identified

Life in one sleek intention,
As if the bright dogs—as if
Brightness itself—had announced

Out loud their dark origins.

A BREED STANDARD FOR THE BORDER COLLIE

Old Magic, useful to the farm, makes work
The eloquence of the place with no
Help from the weather, no high or low

Coutures of the peasant's drudgery —
Picturesque as low dress may be in
Our pricey galleries.   Starvation

Is a drudgery Pip and Gael
Disdain.   Failure is a drudgery
Too; what the collie—intent on what

Eloquence may be got from the sheep—
Desires, is that the proportions should
Matter to the farmer as collies

Find them, for there must be no farm thing
That is not eloquent, no farm thing
That is only that, no rag and fluff

Midden of kindness, no sugar clogged
Affections to excuse imbalance.
A dog with balance and style instructs

The sheep in this chastity for no
Reason beyond the collie's intent
Designs on the beasts, their pastures.

Later the collie takes up love and
Leaves it again to the imbalance
Of heartthrob, the invasionary

Conundrums, the tartish logics of loss.

THE NEW HOUND PUPPY

Now it is time for her name—

Start the call. The time may come
For her job, which is to run
Holes in the palpable wind

Hallowed by world and the world
Will collapse, follow this hound
Through meteoric valleys,

Wolf-shag domains. Here God says
Himself through the wolf until
A slenderness of hound bitch

With a speed like silk shimmers
At God, all arc and angle,
Revelation for voice. So

It was in the beginning
And evermore shall be, so
Her arcs speak back to the light

Which is become an affair
Of luminous shadows, so
It was in the beginning

And evermore shall be in
Her temporal impudence,
Intended as litany.

On moonlit snow the young dog,
Airedale, bred like a furnace,
Makes fantasy strides, his legs

Wide in profile, a pre-Muybridge
Hound in a poem such as
Anyone was permitted

To write, once. This one is fast.
His breeder says he is splendid,
That she isn't sure she dares

Breed another this superb.
His movement so swift and black
He casts a shadow paler

Than he is. Leaps free of it
Tonight and when he pauses
Among other blacknesses,

Crackles of branches and leaves
Left over from last season's
Hurricane, I know easily

Where he is, where the blackness
Is warm, like holes in the ice
Through which spirit fish carol.

Because they are like smoke you
Look and they are not
Looking back but there is still

Smoke in the house and something
Is Wrong! There must not be smoke
In the house. In Virginia

There is Keesha, who slips off
Behind a tree out of reach
Of the heart. You feel your heart

As the hot awkward grab lunge
Sweaty in its palms that she
Says it is in her way of

Slipping away like smoke, but
Unlike smoke leaving behind
No stench, no consolation

Or what appears to console
And does, but only when sure
Evidence of fire, or at

Least heat as answer to
One's own heat, is like solace—
(A hushed pungent incense of

Acknowledgement? of love?) (Go
Try it!   Cry: "Love!" to the place
She never was. She is gone)—

Or——remains, as wit remains
As the innocence of the farm
Grown intellectual for

Wit's sake and not for the filth
Of refusal. The horses,
The old tricolor collie,

Are safe——safe from the deftly
Charged light in the landscape's eyes,
Even the landscape's headlong

Joy beyond joy and even if
She slips past your heart she slips
Cleanly and leaves no damage.

Reasons not to own her are
Reasons to own her if you can
Own up to the quick impact

Of *canis lupus* who is
Never inside except in
Immaculate chastity.

Consider: You and I and the others and Euclid because
the perfect is so hot in us failing to see it below
profane trisections I mean we inherit this sacred
theorem, true, but NOT from that high priest of
ruler and compass FINAL questions seem to cry
from the past If CODINGS of answers without
reverence yield IMPERFECT theories flawed
methods may be INVOCATIONS nevertheless
This chanting WILL SAVE YOU in all of
your visions Behold above the equal
within the inequalities of a mind
that was given after all that I
or that you may see Knowing a
rule is not seeing the form
The restless imbalancings
of the many are our joy
for see from despised
triads inexactness'
very heart arrive
harbingers only
but true ones   Morley's Theorem: The
of the Form   three points of intersection of the
O at last   adjacent trisectors of any triangle form
to have   an equilateral triangle
about
one
1

ALL OF MY BEAUTIFUL DOGS
ARE DYING

My beautiful dogs are dying and
There are others as beautiful if
I am brave enough in my dotage

To face that beauty again, make it mine
In an authenticity of haunch,
Perfection of desire as of that

Young Brittany who, briefly, hunted
Birds and the very essence of bird,
Sharing with me the sky that had been

Able to intend bird, dog, woman,
Desire.   Without the beautiful dogs
No one dares to attend to desire;

The sky retreats, will intend nothing,
Is a ceiling to rebuke the gaze,
Mock the poetry of knowledge.

My death is my last acquiescence;
Theirs is the sky's renunciation,
Proof that the world is a scattered shame

Littering the heavens. The new dogs
Start to arise, but the sky must go
Deeply dark before the stars appear.

A MOSAIC

. . . mais la vision de la justice est le plaisir
de Dieu seul.   —Rimbaud

No violence.   Volunteer gazelles
Nudge against leopards, and they all graze
On air, never waking from our dreams.

Now the mind is a museum. Thus:
Honor to the heart, encompassing
Grateful voles whose measureless gazing

Welcomes all seasons into the earth
Who comforts them after their sojourns.
We welcome the earth, immortal

And faithful as we are, despite death
In the valleys.   Deliberately returning
Itself to us, the earth remains blind

To what we asked for in heedless youth,
Skipping the warning on poems that
We keep these prayers from heat and flame

Lest the hunt begin its conflagrations
Of mind. Now we all live in rapture
And the loss of rapture replaces what

In the gazelle and the leopard,
The mosaics and the museum,
Prefigured grace: that slightest trembling

Of gaze that signaled what was other
Than the perfections of peace. Whence come
The perfections of war. Welcome

Of the earth is still our bitter joy
For there is no lord of hosts for us
(However gallant it is to hope)

Beyond the hope that this past, that sky,
This delicious beauty of a haunch
Or that power of springing up and

Beyond peace, this reach that can only guess
At the pleasure of God as young birds
Guess at air, their scabrous necks craning,

Their heads high, is what we want to be.

NATURAL AND INTENT

The future brings the future
About; the boom swings wide, free
As though with meaning.   If it

Cracks a skull it does or does
Not with sharp, early intent
Marking a path for that sweep

Backward through time.   Words happen
To us or go by, missing
Us by luck or by intent.

The young Airedale flings his pride
Into his bones: He means it
When he prances through the salt

Marsh as if aflame, propelled
By the sweep of pride as birds
Are by the seasons.   And there

By God is what he always
Meant, singular in design,
Loyal from the burning start.

So concentrated become
Wood and meadow and marsh he
Lives in them as if at home.

SOLE LORD

Of life and death? Love
may not even be lord

of love while the wind
draws the grass
to the ice spattered ground

while spring waits
somewhere besides logic

which is where the sun waits
all night, the moon

daytimes, the foal
all winter, the heart

too.
        Love is logic when

Logic draws the foal

up, a wonder of tottering
knowing better than the grasses

to wait for the sun, guaranteed
or not in the silvery edge

thought gives time, the heart
too.

SECOND PERSON SINGULAR

Field mouse, wolf, star, all first;
Second person singulars

Trace across landscapes
That rise for you dear

And trembling for a moment
On the threshold you step through

Safe as houses, other granted
Protections, forbidden ones.

Your feet can curve
Firm with gladness.

Once the Pacific grabbed me out
From an idle swim, and in that unutterable

I learned that you can't curse
The ocean when you need to. Compare: Language

(In which we are like marine fish,
Metabolism right for the brine, and gills)

Is not like the Pacific but moves to
Our outrage, shapes love even

On a rough tongue, sings us
To fine distractions when the waves

Are calm enough. May words evermore be
Only that enormous.

It has been asked, and answers tried out
If that is love there, even
Courage; cat on comforter, dog
At hearth, rounded into comfort whether
After a long run or just a long day
Of comfort and no death visible except,
The usual that, raised in a human paw

These days, hangs over our creatures
That I cannot remember dying in Dickens
Though nations and philosophies did—what if
The word we gave—dumb—opens back separate
Still in unrelated origins and it is not
Their ignorance but rather their silence during

Our slavering climb or no climb at all
That brings us down, and they,
They know this, what
They know. But for us: what if what

They know, they ignore, and that is the silence
Inhabited for us, not pent up
In thrifty rooms?

They know all that other, too,
                              haunches
Carving light at high speeds
And our declarations go after. So should
Our silence.

THE PROBLEM OF DWELLING

I.

Cottages were what was caulked
against the cold, became

through the word's shift
from poor tongues to rich ones

things of summer and shade
a virtue and no progress

was noted even though cats
found warmth as reliable

as ever. What to call it?
Dwelling with you

and you and you and you
and the dog and the cat

in the second person, you
with me in the second person?

In the spaces between
the more than one grammar

we dwell by is an index
of the problem, nothing

I can call it
home by though, winter

and summer dwelling
with the problem. The door is

ajar, and all seasons room
enough for stars and light

to keep the moon alive. Williams

II.

said, "There is no confusion
only difficulty." Only

the problem, like a joy,
moves in the poem as if

there were no blindness
in a snowstorm, as if

our heart-whole hours
were the place of return,

one grammar of persons
fitting the other in order

to fit, understanding
following as it may

as it does and not death,
two people in one hour,

friends or a crowd
knowing the same hour

even with the door ajar; apart
we live and don't

know what to do, true,
but in the rumble of persons

a fit is found and light
to keep the moon alive

FIREPLACES AND SAILBOATS

Next time we build, we say,
the fire will burn

steady accomplishment one end
to the other, waste

prevented if we are
careful, because a fire

is a lot
of things of passage, conservings

so long as it glows
and our sails

never let the breeze
slip by. Timing

is not everything
but time

frames us because
we let it while the gulls

don't even ration joy,
have enough flight, are

allowed by the wind's
abundance. Their

feathers fit every
air but for us it's *This*

time, **this** *time.* We
this time plan the fire

next time, contemplate
the charred log, plan to come about right

next time, contemplate
the empty top gallant but the gulls

immerschon
are the plan of the wind.

St. Luke's eyes are steady on the babe.
I, insufficiently transfixed,
Am led inexorably beyond
Van der Weyden's (you call him Roger,
Just as you ought)—beyond the window
Roger has set behind radiant
St. Luke, peaceful knower, to gardens,
And beyond them
                              to find in the clear
Distance the delicate city street
Where the figures of humanity
Consult the ground, their eyes helplessly
On the details of history that
Hold them there in the street as the laws
Of perspective, not imperfectly,
Hold the infant before the saint's eyes.

It is the beauty of these figures
As background, as reinterpreted
Landscape I cry for; to be landscape
Is not to be at the center, not
The first thing the painter, seizing his
Focus, illuminated, and what
Are we, unilluminated? What,
To go on, is illumination
For? In the painting, for instance,
The atrocity is not in fact
Visible on the streets but in the eyes
Of the painter—St. Luke. The painter,
Gazing only on the bright infant,
Instead of out the window, reaches
A conclusion not plainly implied

In infant glee. Yet St. Luke's face is plainly
Illuminated by what he sees
Directly before him, while I look
Over Roger's shoulder and out the
Window. And weep, to see the city
So delicate and outside, though
I grant the mistake, the mistake of
Weeping, that is, when perhaps I could
Move subtly into the paint and stand
Behind St. Luke. He looks calm enough.

But I, seeing what he sees, would have
No thought of Fridays, or windows, or

Outsides of any sort; this is
The essential weakness of eyes like
Mine, to see, faced with a divine light,
Nothing but divine light, which is why
Landscapes, or whatever you paint
Beyond the garden, become so central,
Not to the conception, which is all
Complete in what the saint sees, but
To the training of the eye that is,
After all, an action of painting

And illuminations. There are those
That descend to the street while the bright
Neon sign above the square that says
True Cigarets glows undiminished
As the hosts of heaven. In Boston,
Standing before this painting I thought,
Even as I was transported, of
Streets in general, the subway ride home,
And the expanse of walks, all crowded,

That lay between you and me at that
Moment. I thought, in short, of you. We

Have Roger to thank for this. With just
The Infant before me I might have
Stepped out of all those streets directly
Into the light — only in my mind,
Of course, thus forgetting the way

Home. As it was I found my way through
The shadows and arrived in your arms
Only slightly bruised, and all because
Roger kindly refrained from making
A portrait of Christ in unrelieved
Brilliance. Light is light. We are guided,
Sometimes, more easily by the faint
Revelations in the shapes shadows
Suggest than by the blank expanses
On the faces of stars. I find some
Guidance, anyway, in my dark fears
Of what lurks in the streets and come to
See the light more clearly because I
Have missed it so many times, many
Hours. Gaze at the ground, then look up,
Is my advice, and see light, at last,
As precious because we find it
In the darkness outside a garden
Between the light and the world.

DISTRACTED IN A CLASSROOM

I was brought up distracted
By pilots and believing

That they all suffered, that some
Were ours, as who wouldn't

Who with her friends named the parts
Of bombers as easily

As wealth's children learned to name
The schools of the mind cradled

In libraries that protect
The names of the histories

Of weaponry. In my case,
In theirs, love sat no colder

In the hall than usual
With decorous songs that rang

With the promise that the song
Of loss was —
                    to be the song!

It was and is exactly
The song of songs, continued

Routing of pigeons from high
Irridescences children

Learn to admire on their wings.
Our colleagues could now converse

About irridescent wings
Or what the song promised them

When they crept out to listen.
And: some of my students, asked

What they always wanted to
Do, reply helplessly, ruffled

Shrugs under sweaters, "To fly.
I always wanted to fly."

They meant without motors, wings,
Or any help from man, god, sky.

We ask aloud, knocking on God: Our last words—
will they be in a familiar language, one
that knows us as a sheepdog
knows her sheep, or at least like a dog with the flock and
against wolves, and just with it too, like Job
with his shepherds?

But that was all before the war
became so huge it overspilled Jerusalem,
all we could say about her and all
Job said too, beseiged by men whose fathers
he would have "disdained
to set among the dogs of my flock!" and our friendship

Was all in what we said about the war
in those days, even before
it broke out, my dear, as though the war
were the wide world sweetened
with goat paths.   One day

The deficiencies of speech grated
oh intolerable and the next day
or so the war swelled even further. We retreated
from our words, which was the way
life went on. Why there is no truth

In the throat of the mob, in the chorus, is
not clear, but your goats are quiet this morning, there
is not to be found truth
in the mob's throat. Here is truth:

Mark the keen grace of seagulls
staggered by swift gusts, how
only in that best of graces cold
is beaten back, mocked
as if by the purposeful slant
away of temporal wings.   Power

Explodes thus and the eyes
flame with rapture; here is the hook
of justice, even in a flock, but there is falsehood
in the mob, the woman casualty
her body protesting with the chorus
just before it tumbled over the bridge, no
truth in the mob; this is a refutation

Of the excluded middleman. Truthless bodies, casual, not up
        to the world
and tumbling.
Stay home and listen
for the telephone on which you will hear
some truth, conference call or no, and when
time proves more interesting
than your heart seek philosophy
apart from the mob because Truth

with nothing to say for herself
hums along with the mob now like a voice
inventing variations—

And the gods—oh Socrates!
      the gods
are unkind to each other and happiness
is the war ethic
that tried me and found me
wanting, as did pity.   Hence: A rubble of broken fossils

trips travelers on their way home, sweepings
of what, withering in the valley, we failed to say, windy threads
that brought the mountains down.   It is enough
to trip a goat, insouciant in the gayest season.   Afterward

poetry is our only kindness
and all our joy when we are ready
to be named again, mistaken again
for the lion rampant with benevolence
at the stern gate.

A brave man, sir. In 1968
He walked through a mine field.

You're not listening. I am
So listening. No,

You're not. This train
Goes through to Berlin and here

We are. Our horses will come later,
When there's time for that and they may
Carry us again on their buoyant backs. We will live,
Here on our side of the Berlin Wall, for horses
Have no interest in skeletons including
Those in the White House, look, Aristotle
Had a reason for writing the way he did, there are
Always the horses at stake. Someone
Must worry about the children's pony, that tough
Hearted little creature whose feet flame and kill him
At the drop of a can of grain. So that's
The job we keep not doing, and how many times
Do you think a pony can die and rise again? But
Don't forget to excuse yourself when you leave
The table to negotiate the long flight of stone stairs
Cut into the hillside. I am trying to say everything
At once because poetry is a hero, poetry
Is a war hero, you're not listening. I am
So listening. No, you're not. Yes I am, those
Stairs, you're talking about the ones you have to climb
Down in order to get to the barn where the hay
Is stored, and you're warning me about not twisting my ankle

On my way to feed the horses, right? And you already told me
All about the manure ring, too slippery in the rain but:
Yes. When you put horses in such an area, tend them
Under an honest sun and they walk
About for years, sometimes galloping, sometimes even prancing
To our touch, the ground becomes flammable.

Yes. Yes. Yes, I am trying to say that the ground
Has become flammable.
                              Excuse me I have to go
Feed the horses. Don't forget the liniment
For Snowbound's bowed tendons, he's the one
Who will do it, from whose back the children
Will catch the brass ring, and they will do this
Whatever we do, but take care of Snowbound's legs
And take care of the children's pony.

In the play, it is an evil policeman in Prague
Who praises the hero. Someone must praise the hero.

The Parts of Light is Vicki Hearne's third collection of
poetry. It follows *Nervous Horses* (University of Texas
Press, 1980) and *In the Absence of Horses* (Princeton
University Press, 1984).

In addition to writing poetry, Ms. Hearne trains and
writes about animals. She is the author of four
nonfiction works: *Adam's Task: Calling Animals by Name*
(Knopf, 1986; Vintage, 1987), *Bandit: Dossier of a
Dangerous Dog* (HarperCollins, 1991), *Animal Happiness*
(HarperCollins, 1994), and *First Friend: The Cultures of
the Dog* (HarperCollins, forthcoming).

Ms. Hearne is also a visiting fellow at Yale University's
Institution for Social and Policy Studies and a contribut-
ing editor of *Harper's*.

This book was typeset in Adobe Perpetua
by the designer, Ann Walston.
It was printed by Princeton Academic Press, Inc.,
on 60-lb. Glatfelter Natural.

The following poems have been published previously: "The Figure 1" in *Advances in Mathematics;* "The Runner and the Mountain," in *The New Republic;* "Comparative Enormity" and "Fireplaces and Sailboats," in *Partisan Review;* "St. Luke Painting the Virgin," in *Raritan* and *Best American Poetry 1992;* "Huck Finn, Credulous at the Circus," "To the Circus," and "Touch of Class," in *Southwest Review;* "Before the War" and "Listening Post," in *The Cresset.*

Library of Congress Cataloging-in-Publication Data

Hearne, Vicki, 1946–
    The parts of light / by Vicki Hearne.
        p.   cm. — (Johns Hopkins, poetry and fiction)
   ISBN 0-8018-4939-X (alk. paper). — ISBN 0-8018-4940-3
(pbk. : alk. paper)
    I. Title.   II. Series.
PS3558.E2555P37   1994
811'.54—dc20   94-10709